Jr. Graphic Mythologies ™

GREEK MYTHOLOGY

Jason and the Golden Fleece

Glenn Herdling

PowerKiDS
press.

New York

To my hero, Mark—may your future be an endless quest of self-discovery.

Published in 2007 by The Rosen Publishing Group, Inc.
29 East 21st Street, New York, NY 10010

First Edition

Editors: Daryl Heller and Julia Wong
Book Design: Greg Tucker
Illustrations: Q2A

Library of Congress Cataloging-in-Publication Data

Herdling, Glenn.
  Greek mythology : Jason and the golden fleece / Glenn Herdling.— 1st ed.
      p. cm.
  Includes index.
  ISBN (10) 1-4042-3396-2—(13) 978-1-4042-3396-6 (lib. bdg.) —
ISBN (10) 1-4042-2149-2 — (13) 978-1-4042-2149-9 (pbk.)
  1. Jason (Greek mythology)—Juvenile literature. I. Title.
  BL820.A8H47 2006
  398.20938'02—dc22
                                            2005037338

Manufactured in the United States of America

CONTENTS

MAJOR CHARACTERS

Jason *(JAY-sen) was the son of Aeson, who was the rightful king of Iolcus. He led the Argonauts on the search for the Golden Fleece. The Golden Fleece was the skin of a golden ram, or male sheep, that had once helped save the life of Jason's cousin, Phrixus.*

Hera *(HIR-uh) was the queen of the Greek gods. She was married to Zeus, who was the king of the Greek gods. Hera was the goddess of marriage and women. She kept women safe when they were having children.*

Aphrodite *(ah-fruh-DY-tee) was the Greek goddess of love and beauty. She was the mother of Eros, who was also a god of love. Aphrodite and Eros helped people fall in love with each other.*

Medea *(muh-DEE-uh) was the daughter of Aietes, the king of Colchis. She had magical powers that she used to help Jason win the Golden Fleece. She also helped murder Pelias, Jason's uncle, by tricking Pelias's daughters into cutting him up into pieces.*

JASON AND THE GOLDEN FLEECE

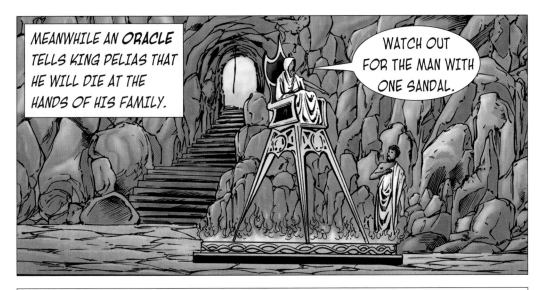

MEANWHILE AN **ORACLE** TELLS KING PELIAS THAT HE WILL DIE AT THE HANDS OF HIS FAMILY.

WATCH OUT FOR THE MAN WITH ONE SANDAL.

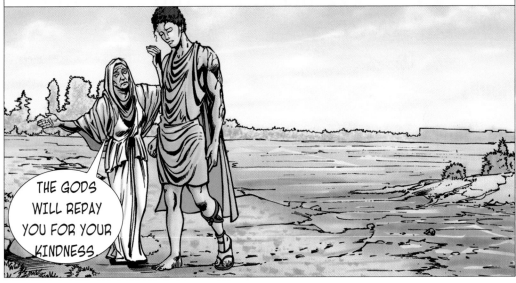

ON HIS WAY TO IOLCUS JASON MEETS THE GODDESS HERA. SHE HAS TURNED HERSELF INTO AN OLD WOMAN. AS JASON HELPS HER ACROSS THE RIVER, HE LOSES A SANDAL.

THE GODS WILL REPAY YOU FOR YOUR KINDNESS

JASON ENTERS IOLCUS. KING PELIAS MEETS THE VISITOR. HE GETS SCARED WHEN HE SEES JASON WEARING ONE SANDAL.

I HAVE COME TO CLAIM IOLCUS AND TO FREE MY FATHER!

WEEKS LATER THE ARGO LANDS ON AN ISLAND. THE GOD HERACLES LEAVES THE SHIP TO FIND A NEW OAR. HYLAS, HIS YOUNG HELPER, GOES WITH HIM.

LET ME COME WITH YOU, MASTER, SO THAT I MIGHT FIND FRESH WATER FOR THE CREW!

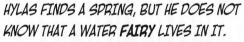

HYLAS FINDS A SPRING, BUT HE DOES NOT KNOW THAT A WATER **FAIRY** LIVES IN IT.

I WISH TO KISS YOU!

NO! I CANNOT BREATHE UNDER—GLUB!

WHILE HERACLES SEARCHES FOR THE MISSING BOY, THE ARGO SAILS WITHOUT HIM.

HYLAS!

ON THE SHORES OF SALMYDESSUS, THE ARGONAUTS MEET KING PHINEUS.

I HAVE ANGERED THE GODS. EACH NIGHT ZEUS SENDS **HARPIES** TO STEAL MY FOOD.

JASON, I WILL TELL YOU HOW TO REACH THE GOLDEN FLEECE IF YOU FREE ME FROM THE HARPIES.

JASON SENDS TWO OF THE ARGONAUTS TO SAVE PHINEUS FROM THE HARPIES. THEY ARE CALAIS AND ZETES, THE WINGED SONS OF THE GOD OF THE NORTH WIND.

THE HARPIES EAT EVERYTHING ON PHINEUS'S PLATE AND START TO FLY OFF. CALAIS AND ZETES FLY AFTER THE MONSTERS AND KILL THEM IN THE AIR!

TO THANK THEM, PHINEUS GIVES THE ARGONAUTS ADVICE.

YOU MUST WATCH OUT FOR THE **CLASHING** ROCKS.

THESE HIGH CLIFFS SMASH AGAINST EACH OTHER IN THE SEA. SEND A DOVE THROUGH FIRST. IF THE BIRD PASSES SAFELY, THEN YOU WILL, TOO.

THE ARGONAUTS SET SAIL THE NEXT MORNING. SOON THEY FACE THE TOWERING CLIFFS OF THE CLASHING ROCKS.

HOW CAN WE SAIL BETWEEN THOSE ROCKS? WE WILL BE KILLED!

TAKE FLIGHT, MY LITTLE WHITE FRIEND. MAY THE GODS GUIDE YOU TO SAFETY!

THE BIRD DARTS THROUGH THE CLIFFS. IT APPEARS ON THE OTHER SIDE UNHURT.

THE ARGONAUTS SAIL TOWARD THE RIVER PHASIS. AT SUNSET THEY REACH COLCHIS, THE LAND OF THE GOLDEN FLEECE.

MEANWHILE ON MOUNT OLYMPUS, THE GODDESS HERA WORRIES ABOUT JASON.

APHRODITE, JASON NEEDS HELP GETTING THE FLEECE FROM KING AIETES.

PERHAPS YOU, THE GODDESS OF LOVE, CAN MAKE THE KING'S DAUGHTER HELP HIM?

MY SON EROS IS MORE SKILLED THAN I AM IN THE ART OF MATCHMAKING.

APHRODITE ASKS EROS TO MAKE MEDEA, THE DAUGHTER OF THE COLCHIAN KING, FALL IN LOVE WITH JASON.

THE NEXT MORNING JASON STANDS ON THE COLCHIAN FIELD AND FACES THE FIRE-BREATHING BULLS.

IGNORING THE FLAMES JASON FORCES EACH CREATURE INTO ITS **HARNESS.**

JASON THEN DROPS THE DRAGON TEETH INTO THE GROUND.

EACH TOOTH QUICKLY GROWS INTO AN ARMED SOLDIER.

JASON THROWS A STONE AT ONE OF THE CREATURES.

THE DRAGON-TEETH MEN TURN ON ONE ANOTHER UNTIL NOT ONE CREATURE IS LEFT STANDING.

KING AIETES IS NOT PLEASED THAT JASON HAS WON.

I SHALL DESTROY THE ARGONAUTS!

THAT NIGHT MEDEA SLIPS AWAY TO THE ARGO.

JASON, YOU MUST GET THE GOLDEN FLEECE AND LEAVE AT ONCE. I WILL HELP YOU!

MEDEA AND JASON CREEP TO WHERE THE GOLDEN FLEECE HANGS FROM A TREE.

MEDEA SINGS TO SLEEP THE DRAGON THAT GUARDS THE FLEECE. SHE AND JASON ESCAPE WITH THE GOLDEN FLEECE. THEY SAIL AWAY ON THE ARGO.

AIETES SENDS HIS NAVY AFTER THE ARGO. THE ARGONAUTS ROW FULL SPEED UNTIL THEY REACH THE SEA AND ESCAPE.

AT LAST THE ARGO RETURNS HOME TO THE HARBOR OF IOLCUS. JASON BIDS **FAREWELL** TO HIS FRIENDS.

THAT EVENING MEDEA SLIPS A SLEEPING **POTION** INTO PELIAS'S CUP. PELIAS'S DAUGHTERS FORCE THEMSELVES TO KILL HIM.

YOUR FATHER WILL BE SO HAPPY TO BE YOUNG AGAIN!

WHEN THE DAUGHTERS ARE DONE, THEY CALL FOR MEDEA TO BRING THEIR FATHER BACK TO LIFE.

MEDEA!

THE WITCH IS GONE! SHE TRICKED US!

JASON'S **REVENGE** WAS DONE.

THE END

FAMILY TREE

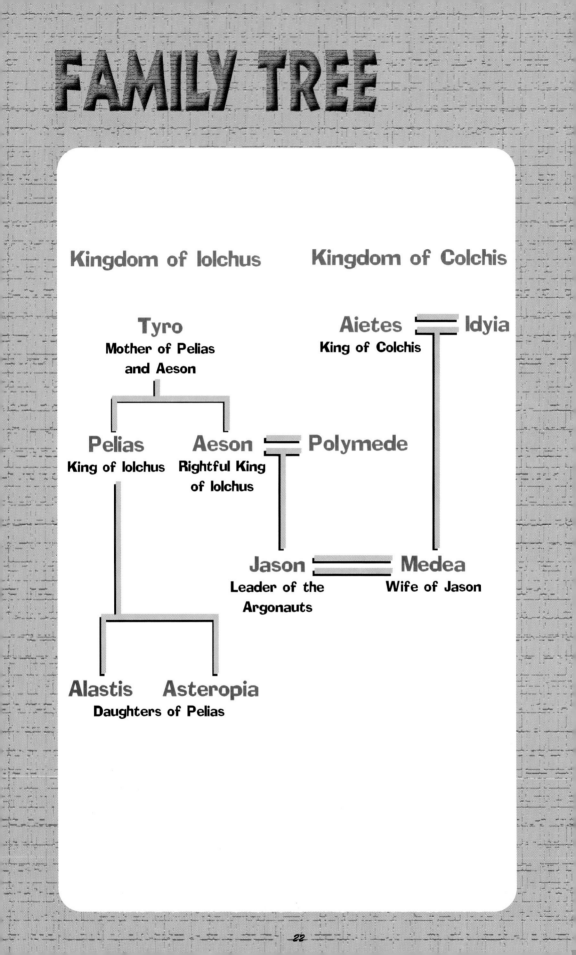

Kingdom of Iolchus

Kingdom of Colchis

Tyro
Mother of Pelias
and Aeson

Aietes
King of Colchis

Idyia

Pelias
King of Iolchus

Aeson
Rightful King
of Iolchus

Polymede

Jason
Leader of the
Argonauts

Medea
Wife of Jason

Alastis   **Asteropia**
Daughters of Pelias

GLOSSARY

centaur (SEN-tawr) A creature that is half man and half horse.

clashing (KLASH-ing) Crashing into one another.

demonstrates (DEH-mun-strayts) Shows how something works.

fairy (FER-ee) A being with magical powers.

farewell (fer-WEL) A way to say good-bye.

harness (HAR-nes) The leather straps, bands, and other pieces used to hitch a horse or other animal to a wagon or plow.

Harpies (HAR-peez) Winged monsters with the faces of ugly, old women and hooked, sharp claws.

ignoring (ig-NOR-ing) Paying no attention to something.

lotion (LOH-shun) A liquid that is put on the skin.

matchmaking (MACH-may-king) Bringing two people together to try to make them fall in love.

oracle (AWR-uh-kul) A person who is able to know things that have not happened yet.

plow (PLOW) To cut, lift, and turn over soil.

potion (POH-shun) A magical liquid.

revenge (rih-VENJ) The act of hurting someone in return for hurting you.

weapons (WEH-punz) Objects or tool used to wound, disable, or kill.

INDEX

WEB SITES

Due to the changing nature of Internet links, PowerKids
Press has developed an online list of Web sites related to
the subject of this book. This site is updated regularly.
Please use this link to access the list:
www.powerkidslinks.com/myth/jason/